DO NOT REMOVE
CARDS FROM POCKET

12/96

ALLEN COUNTY PUBLIC LIBRARY
FORT WAYNE, INDIANA 46802

You may return this book to any agency, branch,

or bookmobile of the Allen County Public Library.

DEMCO

CLOUDLAND

Other books by John Burningham

Borka
The Adventures of a Goose with No Feathers

Trubloff
The Mouse Who Wanted to Play the Balalaika

Granpa

John Patrick Norman McHennessy
—the boy who was always late

Hey! Get Off Our Train

Aldo

John Burningham's ABC

Courtney

Published by Crown Publishers, Inc., a Random House company, 201 East 50th Street, New York, New York 10022. Published in Great Britain in 1996 by Jonathan Cape Ltd.

CROWN is a trademark of Crown Publishers, Inc.

Printed in Hong Kong

Library of Congress Cataloging-in-Publication Data
Burningham, John.
Cloudland / John Burningham. — 1st American ed.
p.   cm.
Summary: While high in the mountains with his parents, Albert falls off a cliff and ends up in Cloudland, where he enjoys playing with the cloud children, but misses his parents.
[1. Clouds—Fiction.] I. Title.
PZ7.B936C1   1996
[E]—dc20   95-49467

ISBN 0-517-70928-7 (trade)
0-517-70929-5 (lib. bdg.)

10 9 8 7 6 5 4 3 2 1

First American Edition

CLOUDLAND

John Burningham

Crown Publishers, Inc., New York

They had spent the day high up in the mountains.
So high were they that they could look at the
clouds below them.

"It's getting late and the light is fading fast," said Albert's father. "We must hurry down before it gets dark."

Then something terrible happened.
Albert tripped and fell off a cliff.

Albert's mother and father looked everywhere,
but they couldn't find him. They were very sad,
because they loved their little Albert.

But Albert was lucky. The children who live in the clouds had seen him falling and said some magic words.

They either said,
"Fumble gralley goggle ho hee,"

or
"Teetum waggle bari se nee,"

or was it
"Gargle giggle fiddle num dee"?

Albert found himself becoming very light, and then the cloud children caught him.

"We'll make you a bed in the clouds, Albert," they said. "You must be tired after your fall."

When Albert woke up the next
morning, the cloud children
had made breakfast.

"After breakfast, we're all going
to climb up those tall clouds
and play jumping games,"
they told him.

Albert enjoyed jumping.
He wasn't at all afraid because he felt
as light as a feather. After the jumping games, they played cloud
ball–but the clouds were becoming
darker and darker.

"There's going to be a thunderstorm.
Let's make as much noise as we can,"
said the children.

Then it began to rain.

"We're going for a swim now, Albert,"
said the cloud children.

After the rain came a beautiful rainbow,
and they all painted pictures until it was
time to go to bed.

The next day there was a strong wind
and they were able to have races.

They raced each other on little clouds,
which was great fun until Albert found
he was being left far behind.

Albert was all on his own.

The other children were drifting farther
and farther away.

Suddenly, there was a terrific noise
and a rush of air, and Albert was nearly
knocked off his cloud.

But the plane left a perfect path for Albert,
and he was able to walk to the other children.

Albert was enjoying his time in the clouds and the games with the children. But one night, as he looked down from his cloud bed, he saw the lights of a city below, and he thought of his mother and father and his own little bed.

"I WANT TO GO HOME," he said.

He said it so loudly it reached the ears of the Queen.

"Now what's all this about?" she said. "Nobody has ever asked to go home from the clouds before."

"I want to be with my mother and father again," said Albert.

The Queen felt sorry for Albert, and she thought for a long time.

At last she said, "I have a plan. It will be difficult, but I'll try to make our clouds drift over where you live."

So while Albert and the cloud children spent their days playing, and Albert slept in his cloud bed each night, the Queen got in touch with the wind.

Until one day she said,

"Albert, tomorrow we'll be over your home. But first we're going to have a party for you, and I've invited the Man in the Moon."

The next evening the clouds drifted over the city
where Albert lived. The Queen and the cloud
children shook hands with Albert and said good-bye.

Then the Queen said the magic words backward.
She either said,

"Hee ho goggle gralley fumble,"

or *"Nee se bari waggle teetum,"*

or was it *"Dee num fiddle giggle gargle"*?

The next thing Albert knew
was that he was back in his own
little bed in his own room and his
mother and father were with him.

Albert sometimes wishes he could
be back playing with the cloud
children, and he tries to remember
the magic words.

People hear Albert saying strange things to
himself–things like *"Nari blooy beany hoo,"*
or *"Meeky magi diddle hee doh,"*
but he can never get it quite right.

"There goes Albert talking to himself,"
they say. "He always did have his head in
the clouds."